THIS BOOK BELONGS TO

children's choice®

Elaine Livermore

Looking for Henry

Houghton Mifflin Company

Boston 1988

Library of Congress Cataloging-in-Publication Data

Livermore, Elaine.
  Looking for Henry.

  Summary: A leopard who bemoans the fact that he
always blends into his background and never gets
noticed finally discovers that spots have their place.
  [1. Leopards—Fiction. 2. Camouflage (Biology)—
Fiction] I. Title.
PZ7.L7399Lm   1988   [E]   88-6868
ISBN 0-395-44240-0

Printed in the United States of America

Y   10   9   8   7   6   5   4   3   2   1

For John, April, and Will

Henry was nice.
He was always pleasant and
sometimes amusing.
But Henry had a problem.
No one ever noticed him.

Even babies and small pets
would not see him.

One day he was hung out
with the wash.

The teacher never knew
when he was in school.

And it was no fun to be
treated like a bedspread.

No one ever paid attention
to him at parties.

Henry had to change something.

One day he got on the bus
to find a place where
he would not be ignored.

He enjoyed the country,
but still no one noticed him.

Henry was taking a nap
when he heard, "Bang! Bang!"

He looked down and saw
an animal hunter.

Henry hoped the hunter
would not see him.

He ran to a village to hide.

The hunter looked and looked
but did not find Henry.

He stood very still so
he would not be noticed.

Henry wanted to go home.

He ran to the nearest bus stop
and waited for the bus.

Back home he was glad he was safe.
He was glad he had not changed.
Henry thought and thought.
"If I can't change, perhaps I
can find a way to use my spots."

One day he saw a sign
for a magic show.

As Henry watched, the magician's assistant began to fall.
The magician was not very good.

Henry quickly ran to help.

The girl floated in the air.

The audience clapped loudly.

Henry helped with
the other acts.

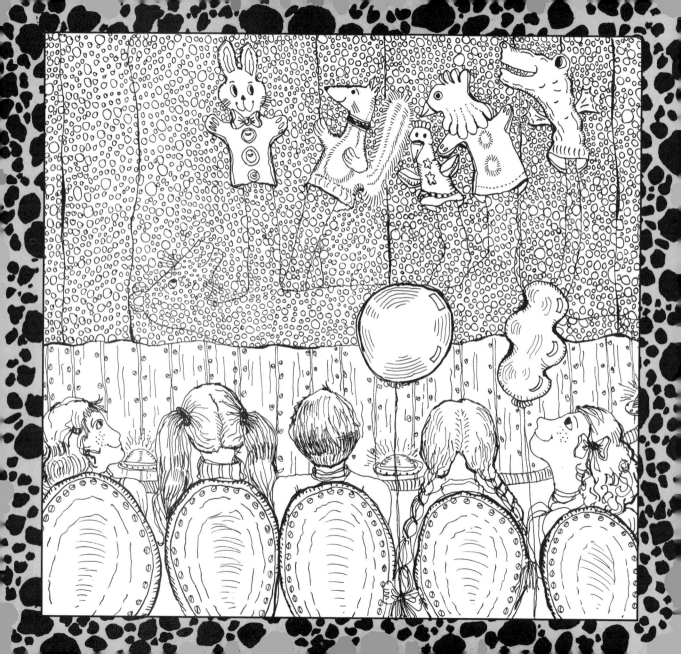

The magician offered Henry a job.
Henry thought,
"Spots have their place too."

From that time on
whenever Henry was invited
to a party, he always put on
a fancy white shirt.